Faith Didn't Die:
A Modern-Day Parable

By Teresa Meyerhoeffer Christensen

ISBN-13: 9798989488407

Bridge2WorldsBooks

5942 Harvest Point Circle

Mountain Green, Utah 84050

www.TeresaMeyerhoefferChristensen.com

Dedicated to

Anyone in need of a little faith…

Including family members and friends who have read a copy of any of my 13 books (a couple have even taken a turn at editing). These supportive souls have stoked my faith in mankind by supporting my dreams of being an author.

Other books by this author:

Ports 2

Ports

The Hero on the Bus Ride Home

Love More Judge Less

A Tale of Three Cities

The Least of 3's

Drought

Hijacking Happiness

There is Love

Not Really Homeless

Seth Row

Angels Unshelved

Have a Little Faith in Me by John Hiatt

When the road gets dark
And you can no longer see
Just let my love throw a spark
And have a little faith in me

And when the tears you cry
Are all you can believe
Just give these loving arms a try, baby
And have a little faith in me

And have a little faith in me
And have a little faith in me
And have a little faith in me
And have a little faith in me

When your secret heart
Cannot speak so easily
Come here darlin', from a whisper start
To have a little faith in me

And when your back's against the wall
Just turn around and you, you will see
I will catch you, I will catch your fall baby
Just have a little faith in me

And have a little faith in me
And have a little faith in me
And have a little faith in me
And have a little faith in me

Well I've been loving you for such a long time girl
Expecting nothing in return
Just for you to have a little faith in me
You see time, time is our friend
'Cause for us there is no end
And all you gotta do is a have a little faith in me
I said a, I will hold you up
I will hold you up
And your love gives me strength in love
So have a little faith in me

Introduction

  I felt impressed several times to write a book about *faith* to add with my two other non-fiction books on *happiness* and *love* since faith is another value I treasure deeply. However, the topic seemed problematic. Each time it came to mind I hesitated at the thought since faith is such an individual experience. Then right before I was about to begin writing *PORTS 3*, the answer came to me after reading *Keturah and Lord Death* for the third time. Faith could be embodied in the story of a girl carrying that name who undergoes an allegorical journey while gaining insights into the actual virtue of faith, sort of like a modern-day parable where individual readers could interpret and glean what they needed for themselves through their own lenses and levels of understanding. I felt giddy at the thought and knew I was ready to begin. The other novel would have to wait. This book is neither non-fiction nor fiction. It is a bit of both, and thus I am dubbing it a parable for the reader to decipher and uncover what is truth. There are layers beneath the obvious. At some point our faith has probably been battered, bruised, or burned, needing intervention or therapies to revive it. Pain is part of earth life and when it surfaces, we must go through some kind of healing process, whether physical, mental, emotional, or all three. For faith to survive we must reach out to someone or something or endure some kind of healing process to help us. Renewing faith often requires faith. Scars may remain, but they are merely evidence that we really lived.

The name of the male nurse character began as Drew after my male nurse nephew with that name. Then one day out of the blue the name *Tergar* came into my mind when I was considering a name for the boyfriend. I had never heard that name before and was not sure where it came from so decided to Google it. My discovery was mind-blowing. I found that the Tergar Meditation Community is a Buddhist meditation community led by a Tibetan meditation master and writer. Tergar (gter sgar) means "encampment of the treasure revealer." Defined: *"Ter" means treasure in the Tibetan language; the practices and wisdom to obtain our greatest potential, alleviate suffering, and attain enlightenment. "Gar" means gathering. "Tergar" then is the place where people assemble to enable transformation.* Tergar needed to be the nurse with a name that connotes depth and powers to heal beyond the physical. It was perfect. Tergar is a Christ-type. Drew was relegated to the boyfriend's name. My Drew is a tall, kind, handsome all-American-looking nephew, so the name fit there too. I also once had a Dr. Cope with a better bedside manner than the physician in this book. Isn't it a great name for a physician? And Faith's last name *Marley* could be a shout-out to the musician who wrote *Don't Worry Be Happy* or to Jacob Marley who had a message for Scrooge, as well as to my beloved Labrador retriever. Many levels amid the levels are buried in this tale.

I began this story on my 64th birthday as a gift to myself since I believe *faith* is the ultimate superpower. Faith can rescue us from our physical, mental, or emotional pain. We all need something to hold on to and believe in. That is what makes life worth living.

Chapter 1

The acrid medicinal smell burning her nostrils woke up Faith first. She could feel her closed eyes beginning to water, but no moisture seemed to spill forth. What in the world was her mother cooking? Or was she still at college in the sorority house? That would make more sense since no one there knew how to cook worth beans or even how to cook beans. Maybe she was still dreaming, and the smell had nothing to do with terrible cooking. Faith's exhausted body felt as if a boulder were pushing her back down into the bed covers, but it had to be about time to rouse herself. She tried to shed the thick sleep. She'd open her eyelids to get herself going, but to her surprise, even with effort, no light entered her world. It must be far earlier than she imagined.

Suddenly, full acknowledgment of intense pain hit her. Every inch of her body hurt. How had she not noticed that before? Her right hand darted to her face to figure out what was keeping her vision dark, but her hand seemed bulky and encumbered without any sensation of touch. Was she wearing gloves? She sent her left hand on a mission to feel her face and found it to be encased in a gauze-like substance. What was going on? Faith tried to sift through the haziness in her brain. She felt drugged. Perhaps she had been drugged. Maybe to deal with all the pain? Massive pain surged through her, making Faith wish she hadn't awakened at all and had stayed hunkered down in the world of dreams where such pain didn't dwell. No way could she go back to sleep now. Where was all the hurt coming from? What had happened to her? She nudged her dulled mind in an attempt to remember.

It was autumn break at the college she attended. Faith had gone home to visit her parents. She remembered going home but nothing after that. She felt 99% positive she was not at home now. The surrounding sounds along with the sharp smells made that clear. This place did not smell or sound like home. An unfamiliar mechanical noise, not one made by her phone, beeped in the background mixed with an intermittent whooshing air-filled sound. Muffed voices could be heard over a distant intercom system of some sort. Was she in an airport? No, she had driven home. But what or who could explain the gauze and pain?

Faith called out calmly, fighting the urge to shriek due to the ever-increasing pain. "Hey, anyone here? Where am I?"

No answer, so she spoke up louder. "Is anyone out there who can tell me what is going on?"

Only machine sounds responded to her unanswered question. The pain, darkness, and unknown were becoming unbearable. Time to pull out the big guns. Faith shouted as loudly as she could through whatever entangled her face.

"HELP ME!"

She could hear a heavy door opening and a female voice speaking above the beeping and whooshing. "You're awake. I'm so sorry, the pain must be terrible."

Still not knowing where *here* was, at least she was not alone and could perhaps get some answers. "Yes, I am hurting…pretty much… everywhere." Faith squeezed out the words through clenched teeth. "Where am I?"

"Let's give you something for pain, poor thing." Faith could hear plastic packaging being opened, followed by a cool substance entering a vein and creeping up her arm as the female voice added, "You're in Kansas City darling, in the Grossman Burn Center." With those locational words, the drugs hit their mark, and Faith escaped into oblivion.

When Faith woke again, she unfortunately remembered where she was but had no idea why or how she got here. Before she had time to call out, Faith sensed a presence stirring at her side. Her ears seemed to have

11

developed super hearing powers to compensate for her bandaged eyes.

"Is someone here?"

Yes, I'm here, can I get you anything, Faith?" The voice sounded an octave deeper. A male was speaking this time, and this voice knew her name.

"Who are you? And yes, more medication would be lovely." Her voice was polite yet tense from the constant and excruciating pain. Faith was not sure if the drugs took away all the agony or just made her not care and allowed her to sleep. As long as the pain was gone, either was fine.

"You are almost due for another infusion of narcotics. My name is Tergar, and I am your nurse on this shift."

"I am ready whenever you are for more sleep juice, but before I go under again can you tell me why I am here and what's happened to me?" Faith was not sure why her eyes were covered. "Am I blind?"

The nurse's response was slow and thoughtful. "You are here, Miss Faith, because you were badly burned. And no, I don't believe you are blind, just bandaged for now."

"How was I burned? And why here, why not at my local hospital?" Faith began to feel frantic.

Again, speaking as if he had all the time in the world, Tergar comforted her with his slow, gentle words. "People who have been severely burned usually require treatment at specialized burn centers. After being provided immediate first aid and wound assessment locally, you were transferred here where you will be provided with the best treatments, medications, wound care, therapy, and possibly surgery when you are more stable."

None of this sounded good. Her nurse had not answered her question about how she had become burned, but Faith was not sure she wanted to know any more at the moment. Just give her the dang painkiller. But no, the male nurse continued speaking.

"The goals of our treatment are to control your pain, remove dead tissue, prevent infection, reduce scarring risk, and help you regain function." Tergar knew this patient would likely need skin grafts to cover her large wound areas, along with months of emotional support and follow-up care, but that was the physician's place to tell her. His job was to keep her comfortable and not scare the badly burned girl whose life had been drastically altered.

"Can I just have the shot now?" Faith could hear his immediate response to her request as he began to prepare her injection.

"*We are twice armed if we fight with faith.*" With her enhanced hearing, Faith heard her nurse speak these words quietly under his breath.

"What do you mean by that comment?"

Startled she had heard him, Tergar explained himself. "Oh, sorry, just some words of Plato that came to mind. Your name may give you an added bonus in your healing."

Faith may not be able to see Tergar's smile, but she could hear it in his voice before sweet, forgiving sleep enveloped her.

Chapter 2

Faith returned to consciousness. She was not sure how many hours had passed, only that the pain had graciously lessened. Now it was barely bearable whereas previously her pain had been off the charts. Her completely dark world had snuffed out any degree of light she had previously taken for granted. She knew where she was and vaguely why she was here. She heard the door open once again as someone entered her space. At least she was never alone for long.

"Hello again, Faith, I need to do a final assessment of your condition before my shift ends." He sounded like the same gentleman who had administered her most recent pain injection.

"How are you doing? Could you tell me the current level of your pain, anywhere between the numbers one and ten, with ten being the highest or worst pain possible?"

How does one put a number on their pain? She would try. "Well, earlier it was like an eleven or twelve, but now maybe an eight. It is still bad, but I can almost stand it."

"I am sorry, Faith. I'm afraid it is going to be bad for a while. We need to stay on top of it and keep it under a ten to ensure you can handle it and not let it get out of control. Five or less is the goal for now."

"That would be great. Thank you." Memories of his last pre-shot visit in her room returned. "By the way, what were you saying about my name before I drugged out?"

"Oh, just thinking about what a perfect name you have for all you are going through at the moment. Absent-minded me spoke my thoughts aloud. Sorry."

"No, it's okay. I guess I'd never really thought much about my name before. My mother said she named me Faith Hope because the two words go hand in hand since *faith* is things *hoped* for that cannot be seen."

"Sounds like a wise woman."

"Yes, she is, and right now I cannot see, so it is eerily appropriate." Faith did not see the grimace spreading across Tergar's face at her response. "My parents had a hard time having children, so they used IVF (In Vitro Fertilization). It took them like seven tries to get me, so I was named before I was born." Had this guy given her a truth serum? She was sharing more than she was usually comfortable sharing, but it helped distract her from the pain. "I guess they wanted to give me a powerful name to help me stick around. It was their last try to have children. I am their one and only."

Her parents were believers; Faith was a believer too, but just not sure exactly what she believed in. Maybe she was about to find out. "Can you tell me more about what is going on? Why aren't my parents here? Do they even know what happened to me?"

"The doctor will be in later today to go through everything with you. I am only here to assess your health needs and keep you comfortable. If we cannot get your pain down to a low enough level with medication, would you be willing to try any alternate type of therapy? Pet therapy wouldn't be allowed yet, due to the risk of infection. You're in isolation and it's difficult to gown up a dog." Tergar was not sure the patient had picked up on his lame attempt at humor, but he felt relieved he had so adeptly switched topics. He was not prepared to share any more tragic news with this badly burned patient. "Music therapy can be soothing and might help if you'd like to give it a try."

Faith wondered what being in isolation looked like and why this nurse was being so stingy with details. Realizing perhaps he didn't know anymore, she merely asked, "You mean like giving me a radio or something to listen to?

"There are channels on the television in your room that play calming sounds of nature or soft instrumental music. Also, various musicians volunteer time each day to play their instruments for patients upon request."

"Sure, either would be a nice diversion. Can I have more pain medication too, please?"

"I think it is close enough to the scheduled time to be alright. We will set you up with a PCA pump soon so you can control dosing your own medication."

"You trust me to do that? How do you know I won't overdose?"

"It is safe. With patient-controlled anesthesia, you don't need to wait for a nurse. You can get smaller doses of pain medicine more frequently to stay on top of your pain. You cannot give yourself too much because it is calibrated."

Faith had never heard of such a thing. More questions than answers filled her head in this place.

"I am looking forward to seeing you tomorrow, Miss Faith, hang in there. Remember, *Faith is the bird that feels the light when the dawn is still dark.*"

Faith heard the door shut behind "her" philosophical nurse as the sounds of a distant waterfall filled her room, and more of the sweet painkiller entered her veins. Did she hear a bird too? Was it coming from the sounds on the TV or was it the bird Nurse Tergar had talked about? His bird could feel the light in the darkness. Faith only felt blindness in the darkness. She would have to save her unanswered questions for the doctor. After all, what did she know and what could she remember? Not much.

Growing up, Faith had felt the pressure of fulfilling her parent's dreams as an only and cherished child. They adored their bright-eyed, tow-headed little girl. Her mother French-braided her hair in the most unique ways, and her father took her fishing on Saturdays. She had been a good girl and tried to do everything right. Her parents were more forgiving of her mistakes than she had been. She had girlfriends, but in high school Drew had become her best friend. The two of them were still close, but she had gone away to college, and her handsome high school star athlete boyfriend had stayed home to run the family business. Faith had chosen to be a mathematics major in college. Math was finite, tangible, and easy to wrap her mind around, not like loosie-goosy psychology where most of the answers were nebulous. Her thoughts pinged everywhere. Faith knew she was a good student, even better than good because she had graduated salutatorian in her high school class. She also loved music so was glad her nurse had suggested music therapy. She remembered considering music as her field of study, but being too practical she recognized that music wouldn't pay the bills. Knowing she was not rockstar material, music had become her hobby. She loved to play the piano and guitar but was not sure her hands and fingers would ever be able to fly lightly over the keyboard or strings and create melodies again, especially in these bandages.

These thoughts brought her to the here and now. Faith remembered enough that she must not have amnesia. But what had happened to her and where were her parents? As the effects of the drugs hit her system, Faith's thoughts became even fuzzier, but she wanted to remember. She needed to remember. She had come home on fall break. Yes. What next? Obviously, a fire had occurred. But what fire? Where? When? As the medication helped Faith slide again into oblivion, her mind filled with images of the fire. Her house, the house she had grown up in, the house where her parents still lived–all had been devoured in flames. And she and her parents had been inside the burning house.

Chapter 3

A nightmare of flames had engulfed Faith before she awakened herself. Not even her sleep was a safe place anymore. She could sense from the voice that a man stood before her. The voice was even deeper than her nurse's and came from a higher elevation than his. This man seemed to be older, taller, and more businesslike.

"Good morning, Faith. I am Dr. Cope. I have visited you before now, but you were not alert enough to process it. Please know your recovery is coming along well under the circumstances. I have been told you have some questions for me."

"Yes, those questions have mostly to do with my 'circumstances.' I need to know what happened. I don't remember much. I know I am badly burned, but that is about it." Faith, now wide awake, was ready for answers.

"Yes, you were badly burned in a house fire."

"How badly? Besides the constant pain, I know nothing. What does this mean for me, and how are my parents? I know they would be here if they could. Are they in this hospital too?"

The physician took his time to answer. "You have been burned over a large portion of your body, much of your torso, neck, part of your face, along with one of your arms and hands. Your legs and feet are relatively burn-free. What that means as a general guideline is that you should plan on staying in the hospital one day for each percent of burn coverage. For example, if you were burned over 25% of your body, you could anticipate being in the hospital for 25 days. You have been burned on nearly 50% of your body surface, so you should plan to be here longer. The size and depth of your burns and the complications that may arise can lengthen your time in the hospital, so two months is a reasonable estimate. Let me explain the procedures you might expect during that time."

Faith liked math, but this was ridiculous. She could be here for two months, and now he was going to tell her the medical care plan before saying anything about her parents' condition. She hoped they had fared better than she had. "Please, first I need to know about my mom and dad."

"I would like to change your dressings and explain your treatment plan before we have that discussion."

"I won't be able to hear or process any of what you say until I know about my parents."

"I understand." The tall doctor she imagined standing before her in some color of scrubs took a deep breath before proceeding. "I am very sorry to inform you that your parents did not survive their injuries. From what I know, they both received more smoke inhalation than you, but they did not have your youth and vitality to battle the damage to their bodies. Your mother passed away in the fire at the scene, and your father succumbed a day later in the hospital. I will give you a few minutes to digest this information and come back after I see my next patient. I plan to remove your bandages and to check your healing progress."

Just another day at the hospital for this man of science, but Faith's whole world— as well as her body— had burned to the ground. She didn't even care if he came back to check anything. Let her rot in this bed wrapped as a mummy. She felt as if she had begun the mummification process already. Faith's despair was too deep to even cry. Her grief had encased all sound. There was not only a pit in her stomach; her whole being had fallen into the pit, and she did not know if she could ever get out. The two people who had given her life and loved her unconditionally from birth were gone. She no longer had her biggest cheerleaders when she needed them most.

An indeterminant time later, another presence entered the room. It was not the doctor. He had sent a replacement to finish his tasks after dropping the fatal bomb on her. Faith was not ready to climb out of her misery, but a kind, semi-familiar voice roused her from her dark well of sorrow.

"Miss Faith, I am here to change your dressings if that would be alright." Stab her in the heart for all she cared. Faith felt nothing. It was as if she did not exist.

When she did not respond, Tergar continued. "I heard you have just received the most terrible news. I am very sorry. You don't have to speak to me if you prefer. I will just tend to my duties. Know I am here and that I care." Tergar continued to speak aloud as he worked.

"I am removing the dressing from your face. We only use dry gauze here at the burn center. You may feel a little resistance and encounter a rush of light that will feel extremely bright after having had your eyes covered."

Faith barely felt the tug on her raw dermis as her nurse removed layers of bandages. Yes, the light overpowered everything. She could definitely see but had to close her lids against the bright onslaught. Nurse Tergar's gentle voice rambled on, sharing instructions which she caught only snippets of here and there as she adjusted to the light.

"You will begin receiving water-based treatments soon with ultrasound mist therapy to clean and stimulate the wound tissue. Hopefully, that won't be as painful. The fluids you are receiving through intravenous infusion are to prevent dehydration and organ failure. Then we will keep on top of the pain and anxiety with medication, particularly before your dressing changes. Healing burns can be incredibly painful." Tergar graciously didn't seem to expect her to answer. It was as if he knew she couldn't handle one more responsibility right now, so he was taking care of all the conversation himself along with her wound care.

"If you develop an infection, you will need IV antibiotics, so let's keep your healing baby-soft new skin clean, shall we? Your doctor may recommend a tetanus shot, and eventually we will get PT and OT involved as needed. Since the burned area covers some of your joints, you will likely need physical therapy exercises. They will help stretch the skin so your joints can remain flexible. And occupational therapists will help if you have any difficulty doing your normal daily activities." He was spewing a wealth of information when all Faith really wanted was the calm verbal cadence of someone who cared. "Are you ready to open your eyes so we can check your vision?"

Faith wasn't sure she was ready. If she could not see anything more than flashes of light on top of dealing with her mangled body and other insurmountable losses, she may never get out of this bed. Slowly, she slid her eyelids open just a slit. Color mingled with the light as forms began to take shape. A blurry figure stood before her. His outline appeared to be of average height and girth. Faith blinked her eyes a few times in an attempt to gain greater focus. Jet-black hair topped the figure's head, but the features beneath his caramel-colored skin were still difficult to make out clearly. His smile revealed bright white teeth.

"There you go, that's my girl. Can you tell me what you can see?"

Faith wasn't sure she wanted to answer so merely said, "You, I see you."

"Good, I hope that's good anyway." Tergar continued to smile but didn't push the girl for more. He merely replied, "*Be faithful in small things,* oh Faith-full one, *because it is in them that your strength lies.*" He would wait to let her see her own image another day. One shock at a time was enough for this devastatingly injured girl.

"Music therapy volunteers are waiting outside your room to play for you when I am finished. Just relax and enjoy their melodies as much as you can."

Faith didn't want to see anyone, and no one needed to see her. She was glad they couldn't come into her room. Suddenly, without any warning, fear's icy fingers wrapped around her heavy heart, and she felt afraid. Afraid to look in a mirror, afraid to live life without her mom and dad. Who will walk her down the aisle? If her face and 40% of her body are scarred and disfigured, will anyone even marry her? Future children will never feel their grandparents' unconditional love. Waves of never-before-experienced sadnesses washed over her. She knew volunteers waited outside, hoping to soothe and heal her devastated soul. She was heartbroken, but she was not rude, and it would be wrong to ignore them or ask them to leave. For all she knew, music therapy might help.

Strains of soft instrumental music filled her sterile room. Faith recognized Debussy's *Clair de Lune* followed by Grieg's *Morning Mood* from Peer Gynt. It was actually quite relaxing. She heard strings and a flute, perhaps a violin–no the sound was too elegant–it must be a harp. Perhaps she had joined her angel parents. The music made her forget and remember at the same time. However, right now, Faith's favorite part of her dismal world was the meds which brought her an all-forgetting sleep. Yes, she would do her therapy and burn treatments begrudgingly, and the music therapy was nice with its hidden beauty and symmetry amid the sterile environment. Music added color, and with that final thought, Faith fell fast asleep.

Chapter 4

Days crept by, gaining a rhythmic flow from Faith's medical routine of endless dressing changes, treatments, and various therapies. Burn Center personnel paraded throughout the unit, each with their own tasks to perform. Due to low staffing and scheduling issues, the hospital assigned Nurse Tergar to care for Faith almost daily and with double shifts on some days. He continued to share insights along with a *faith* quote of the day as he performed his duties. Today, during painful hydrotherapy he used warm running water to gently cleanse and help the healing process by softening and removing dead tissue, enabling new healthy tissue to form. After it was over, Tergar pulled from his hat a nearly perfect quote.

"To have faith is to trust yourself to the water. When you swim, you don't grab hold of the water because if you do, you will sink and drown. Instead, you relax, and float."

Faith pretended not to be impressed, but she could not keep an involuntary smile from trying to turn up the corners of her taunt lips. As she wondered how her patient caregiver had been able to come up with all these quotes, Faith could not help but be slightly inspired by his literary efforts.

"You know, you will be out of isolation before much longer and be allowed guests. Do you think you are ready to take a gander at yourself before others get the chance?"

Faith had not yet surveyed the damage done to her face and had asked that all mirrors in her room be covered or removed. She'd also avoided seeing her reflection in windows and other reflective glass or screens. She did not feel ready to have visitors see her either, especially Drew. She wondered if her boyfriend had tried to visit her or if he thought she had died along with her parents since she hadn't heard from him. That would be tragic. Trying to be positive, she gave Drew the benefit of the doubt that he may not know she was here in the burn center, only a few hours away from their hometown. Or maybe he wanted to give her time to recover. It did cross her mind he might need time to gather his own courage before seeing her, but she didn't want that thought to linger for any length of time, so she buried it.

Drew was her classically handsome, all-American-looking significant other with unruly blonde hair and bright blue-green eyes. Faith's thoughts turned to her sweetheart, a gifted athlete in whatever sport he played who had a huge, kind heart to match the size of his shoulders and chest. No, if he knew she was here he would be here. Drew and Faith had dated since high school, and he was crazy mad about her. As the love of Faith's life, Drew insisted he was willing to marry her whenever she was ready. Would she ever be ready now?

"I guess I cannot avoid all reflective surfaces forever. How long do I have? Can I refuse all visitors? That is if any come to see me."

"You are progressing so well. I'd say in the next few days you will be downgraded to partial isolation at least. Guests may still have to mask up and wear gowns, but they should be able to come into your room.

"Please, don't lie to me, is it really bad? My face I mean. Will it freak people out? I can see most of the rest of me, well, not my back, but I know how crispy my chest and arm are. Tell me."

"I have seen worse."

"That isn't saying much. You work at a burn center, for heaven's sake. Prepare me, please."

"There has been a lot of damage, especially to the right side of your face and neck. It will be startling at first, but plastic surgery can do amazing things with reconstruction today."

"Reconstruction! That's not comforting. Maybe you're too honest."

"Expectations make all the difference. You asked to be prepared."

"Give me a dang mirror, let's get this over with."

"Are you sure?"

"No, I'll never be ready, so I might as well pull off the metaphorical Band-Aid along with this burnt skin."

Tergar turned off the water therapy and gently patted the raw skin partially dry before producing a small hand mirror from a nearby drawer. "Remember this is ground zero. It is all up from here."

"And inner beauty is what is most important, I know, I know." Faith may not have had a leading lady's or film star's good looks, but she knew she was an attractive girl."

Tergar gently held the mirror up for Faith to gaze into, but nothing her nurse had said prepared her for what she saw. An involuntary gasp escaped. Pinkish-red welts textured most of the right side of her face and neck which would be difficult to cover up now that much of her hair on the same side of her head had burned or melted away. An inch-long section of her lower right lip, a chunk of her nose the size of her thumb, and her entire right eyebrow had vanished. Blessedly, her eye had been spared, but the damaged lid did not fully cover the eye. Faith fought back tears that tried to fill her eyes, but only the left one felt damp. Her right tear duct must be damaged as well.

"Looks like I'll be needing a mask to cover half my face like the good ole' Phantom of the Opera." Even her attempt at humor came out stiff and scarred. "You didn't do my new look justice I'm afraid. I'm freaking hideous."

"I'm sorry, the first time is always a shock. I didn't know you before, but you are still a beautiful girl. You will get used to it."

"I don't want to get used to it. I want my face back." Faith shrieked louder than she intended.

"You will meet others here and hear their stories. Life won't seem as bad, I promise."

"I don't want your promises. I want you to get out of here. I don't want anyone to see me like this. No visitors please, especially no one named Drew."

Tergar dropped his hand holding the mirror and left Faith in her room without sharing a clever faith quote on his way out. He'd give the actual Faith time to adjust to her new reality in the privacy of her own space for a little while. He would check in on her again before his shift was over. It sounded like she had not yet received the final piece of painful news that would be coming. This girl needed a break or at least something solid to hold onto. Tergar could tell Faith was a fighter, but even Mohammad Ali had his limits.

Chapter 5

Dr. Cope stood before Faith this morning. Her initial assessment of him when her eyes were still bandaged turned out to be correct. Taller than Tergar, the doctor was slim with a much more professional appearance than her nurse. From his closely cropped salt and pepper immaculately groomed hair, she thought he might be in his forties. He was even wearing the scrubs she had pictured and she would not be surprised if he owned a different color for every day of the week. Today's set was aquamarine or turquoise. She was never quite sure of the name for each shade of blue-green.

"I heard you have some concerns about your appearance, Miss." The doctor looked down at the chart and then added, "Marley."

"You might say that, look at me." Faith withdrew her hands from in front of her face. She had not even been allowed to drape a scarf over her head.

"I initially informed you to give us two months, and you may need a few follow-up surgeries afterward. Patience. You may never look exactly like you did before your injury, but you will fit into polite society just fine. I assure you. We are even able to do full face transplants today, but you are far from needing that much intervention."

Was this supposed professional caregiver for real? He sounded more like a relative of the fictitious Dr. Frankenstein. Dr. Cope's bedside manner needed vast improvement. Hopefully, his skills as a physician were stellar to compensate for his appalling lack of empathy. "Let's just say that I'm discouraged doctor and not ready to have anyone see me like this. Obviously, I would have let my parents see me, but that is no longer an option." She knew she would start crying again if she talked about them any longer so changed the subject. "I especially do not want a person named Drew Michaels in to see me yet. Could you please make a note of that on my chart?"

"That is understandable. The male nurse, the darker-skinned one, mentioned something to me about your situation. I believe he has been looking into the man named Drew. You will need to ask him more about it."

The darker-skinned one? The doctor didn't even know Tergar's name. How disgusting. "Okay, yes, I will do that when I see him." She would much rather talk to Tergar anyway.

"I have seen him in the halls this morning. You should have your opportunity soon enough. Do you have any more questions that I can answer?"

Faith had many more questions but would not give this man the time of day. He certainly was not in tune enough to understand what she was going through. "Not right now. I will let you know if I have anything that Tergar, the nurse you mentioned, cannot answer for me." Faith knew that possibility would be highly doubtful. Dr. Cope exited immediately, leaving Faith to wonder what Tergar was looking into about Drew. She did not need to wonder long.

"Good morning, Faith-full one." Tergar, the supposedly darker nurse, entered her room bringing sunshine with him.

"Have you been stalking me on social media?" Faith did not wait to ask.

"What?"

"The doctor, the one with ice running through his veins, said you had been checking out Drew."

Tergar stifled a chuckle about her description of Dr. Cope. "Dr. Cope is very proficient at what he does, but he's definitely not one to waste time chatting. He didn't tell you anything about your friend?"

"No, he said you would."

There was no use dragging this out, but Tergar hated to be the one to give Faith more bad news. "I wondered why you wouldn't want him to visit, so I looked to see what I could find out without prying. I wasn't trying to be a stalker, just wanted to be able to care for your emotional needs as well. It seems like you two were very close."

"Yes, we are. We've been together for four years. What did you discover?"

"There is no easy way to tell you this, Faith. It seems your friend, a true, gallant gentleman, went into your house to save you from the fire. He did save you, but then he went back in to find your parents and never made it out. I am so sorry. He sounds like an amazing human being."

"What? What are you saying? Drew was in the fire too? He didn't make it out? That cannot be right. Why would you tell me something that terrible?" A feeling of panic began to swell inside Faith.

Tergar knew that nothing he could say or do would make this news any better or spare Faith one of life's brutal knockout blows. Faith knew the truth; she just did not want to accept it. He knew the grieving process is different for every person. He would not rush her. "Drew gave you the most he had to give. He gave you your life. Knowing how much your parents meant to you, he valiantly tried to save them for you. He sacrificed his life in the process."

"I don't want my life without any of them in it!" Faith screamed. The love of her life had died rescuing her and trying to save the rest of her family from the fire. Now Faith really did want to die. She could not understand why she alone had lived. Was Drew really gone? The Drew who wanted to marry her? If so, that would never happen. Faith had cheated Drew out of fulfilling his future dreams, dreams that were now buried with him. "WHERE IS HE!"

"I am so sorry. He has been buried, Faith. His family and friends held a funeral for him, but they are planning a celebration of life at a later date."

A celebration of life? His life had been cut short by her. "I cannot do this. Just let me die. Please." She had already stopped breathing anyway. Death would just make her condition official.

For the next several days, Faith stopped eating. What was the point? She had pulled out the annoying IVs keeping her alive a few times, but it was futile. Someone always kept putting them back in. Tergar had been trying his hardest to find ways to break through the darkness and suffocating gloom in her world. Today his quote had been "*Faithless is he that says farewell when the road darkens.*" Then he asked her if she had ever read J. R. R. Tolkien. When she didn't respond, he went on.

"I'll bring you a copy of *The Lord of the Rings*. Sometimes heroes die, but it is part of their mission. It means they truly lived. All of life is a treacherous journey Faith, but that does not mean our stories cannot have a happy ending."

"I'm not expecting a happy ending; I just want an ending. An ending to the pain, the loss, the remembering." Faith turned over, away from Tergar to face the wall. "Leave your book if that will make *you* feel better." She knew she would not be turning its pages anytime soon.

Chapter 6

Faith woke from a vivid dream that felt more real than any dream she had ever had. She was traveling down a long dark tunnel. She felt no pain, and her skin was as smooth as her formerly flawless complexion. However, other obstacles blocked her path. Dirty water smelling of rank sewage, somewhere between the size of a modest river and a moderate stream, flowed down the tunnel with cat-sized rats swimming in the swill and dotting its shores. Faith could see light at the end of the tunnel and a personage standing there waiting for her. Determined, she pushed on through the gross filth and challenging circumstances. As she came closer, she recognized Drew standing there, smiling as handsome and perfect as ever with his blonde locks glowing in the light. They engaged in a conversation she could only recall parts of now.

"I thought you were dead."

"Do I look dead to you?" Drew teased her with his impish grin.

"But what about the fire?"

"Oh, that. I have moved past and am waiting here for you."

"Let me come to you right now." Weaving through the deepening water while avoiding the vermin, Faith tried to forge ahead.

"You cannot come yet, my dearest Faith. If you do, my sacrifice to save you would be worthless. You need to live a long life for both of us. There is much for you to do."

"But I love you. I'm so sorry I delayed marrying you." Actual tears ran down her face.

"No regrets. You will love again, and I will be here when it is your time to return."

"But how could you ever want me when I look like this?"

"I only see your beauty. Everyone here is glorious and seen through a lens of love."

"Please, Drew, let me join you."

"I will be close..."

Abruptly, she woke up. The pain had returned. Drew was nowhere, but she could still smell his aftershave: a mixture of musk and sandalwood. Even in the purified isolation air, it lingered. Maybe it hadn't been a dream. Faith felt horrified she had forgotten to thank him for saving her and wondered if she could find him again if she went back to sleep. In her heart she knew he wouldn't be there. What could she do to get him back?

Before Faith had time to fully analyze and absorb the impact of her dream, two other groups of visitors entered her quarters. A couple of police officers had decided she was well enough to answer a few questions concerning the fire. Their investigation had almost ruled out arson, but they wanted to ask if she was aware of anyone who might want to do her family harm. Faith assured them no one she knew could do something so heinous, and her parents had no enemies she was aware of. Under the circumstances, they concluded it was an unfortunate accident. 'Unfortunate accident' seemed too casual to describe an event that had caused the loss of three lives.

The law enforcement investigators did leave Faith with the best news she had received since this whole nightmare had begun. Their family Sheltie, Cicero, had survived the fire and was waiting for Faith in temporary foster care placement until she had a home to take him to. The thought made Faith's life feel slightly worth living. Cicero could be her therapy dog. Tergar would like him. A famous quote from the original Cicero of Rome, "*Faithfulness and truth are the most sacred excellences and endowments of the human mind,*" would fit right in with Tergar's quotes on faith. Strange that she would even care if her nurse liked her dog.

On the heels of the law officers, her less-than-favorite doctor decided to pop in to update her on her care plan. He always left the impression of a stern teacher or taskmaster in his wake.

"I will give you the good news first, Miss Marley. You have been lucky to not need breathing assistance of any kind. Burns on the face or neck can at times cause the throat to swell shut. If that appeared likely, we would have needed to insert a tube down your trachea to keep oxygen supplied to your lungs. You have also been spared a feeding tube for nutritional support, and we have not had to ease blood flow around your wounds. When a burn scab surrounds a limb, it can tighten and cut off the blood circulation. One that goes completely around the chest can make it difficult to breathe. I have not had to cut an eschar to relieve pressure.

However, it appears you will need skin grafts. Tomorrow, I will perform a surgical procedure in which sections of your own healthy skin will be used to replace some of the scar tissue caused by the deepest burns. Donor skin from deceased donors or pigs can be used as a temporary solution, but I plan to take skin from your inner thighs. It is best to do this within the first few weeks. In around seven percent of cases, the skin graft fails to attach to the wound site, and a re-grafting procedure may be necessary. There is also the option of using skin flaps where the blood supply is intact instead. Flaps are sometimes thought to provide better cosmetic results than skin grafting because the skin tone and texture are usually better matched. Additionally, they have a reduced chance of failure in comparison to skin grafts. With a flap, larger amounts of tissue can be used, including muscle if required. Some reconstructions need both a flap and a graft. After this initial surgery, a plastic surgeon will take over to improve appearance and flexibility. They may decide to use some flaps instead of grafts."

Faith just listened. Dr. Cope did not seem to require her input on the topic but rambled on sharing all his expertise. The man did seem knowledgeable. She was glad he was at least competent since any attempt at verbal comfort was missing. An emotional hug of some kind would have been nice since a physical one probably wasn't allowed.

Tergar came in later that evening to begin prepping for her for surgery in the morning, the first of many surgeries it sounded like she would need to be whole again. His unhurried manner and gentle presence made it easier for her to open up and share inner thoughts pressing on her mind.

"I saw Drew in a dream, but he wouldn't let me come to him."

"Did the dream give you any comfort?" Tergar showed interest but didn't press her.

"I'm not sure. It was wonderful to see him, but why couldn't I go to him? What could that mean?"

"I cannot say for sure, Faith Hope, but remember that *Faith is an oasis in the heart which will never be reached by the caravan of thinking.* Open your heart and feel your way on this journey to him or wherever it may take you. We cannot rush our fates. In the meantime, you might as well decide to live.

Perhaps she would take Tergar's most recent message on faith into her dreams tonight as she tried to find her way back to Drew again.

Chapter 7

Back in her room following the grafting procedure, Faith experienced new pain radiating from her formerly pain-free leg region. You couldn't really call it pain by comparison, more like discomfort. This level of hurting was much lower than what she felt over the burned areas. Hopefully, thigh skin would look good on her arm and chest. Doctor Cope told her an excellent plastic surgeon would handle the grafts on her face as soon as she was stable from this surgery. So much to look forward to, she thought sarcastically.

Faith knew she often acted in a gruff and dismissive manner toward her caregivers. Most avoided her room unless assigned there, but even then, they kept their interactions as brief as possible. The only one who didn't seem to give up on her no matter how onery she was toward him was Tergar. He continued to share insights as he tended to the scars not only on her tender new skin but also on her fragile heart. Of course, he was the nurse assigned as her caregiver after the surgery. This guy must be a glutton for punishment, and today she would crush even his chipper attitude.

"Good morning, gorgeous Faith. It sounds like the grafting went very well. Just so you know, the donor area on your legs should only take about five to ten days to heal. The areas are quite small and were closed with tiny stitches. The color of your new skin may appear red or purple at first, but it will begin to look more like your surrounding skin over time. When the bandage is removed, your graft may look crusted and discolored. This is normal and okay. The newly located skin will change color over time and be as good as new or as good as your old skin. Know that it may look very red for two to three months, so don't worry because the color will eventually fade."

"Would you stop with the good guy routine and always being so nicey, nicey; you have no idea what I am going through." Faith nearly screamed at her untiring angel of mercy.

"You are correct, Faith. No one can fully understand another person's pain." Tergar paused and took a long look at her as if searching into her soul. "However, you are not the only person to have survived very hard things. I am going to tell you a story." Tergar's life had not been a picnic, but he didn't want to make it a competition. He just wanted to give the girl some perspective. His life experiences had taught him what he now knew. Life is but a journey and he had gained vast treasures of knowledge along the way.

"I grew up in Vietnam. My mother was of Eurasian descent from the combination of her parents, a local Vietnamese girl and an American GI who went home after the war leaving my grandmother with my mother, Tuyen, in her belly."

Faith noticed Tergar had a slightly exotic look with a hint of something foreign in his genetic background, but she didn't want to interrupt him and stop the flow of his story. How had she missed that before? It was obvious if one looked at him. Even Dr. Cope had called him the dark one.

"Tuyen means angel in Vietnamese, and my angel-mother now lives in heaven along with your parents. Never accepted by her people due to her mixed-race genetics, she had to find ways to support herself however she could. She also ended up with an unplanned baby, me, the product of her pregnancy. I look more Caucasian than my mother since I'm just a quarter Vietnamese and half something else. She never knew who my father was, or if she did, his name died with her. Her life was hard, and she passed away before I was four years old. My grandmother who raised me did remember the name of my GI grandfather. She said it was something a woman didn't forget. So, when I was old enough, I left Vietnam in search of Sergeant Mace Flint. It was a tall task, and I am not sure why I thought I could find the man, but I did. Agencies in the United States are set up to help and make up for the horrors left behind in my former country after the war. However, Sergeant Flint was less than thrilled to meet a grandson he did not know existed and refused to accept I could be any relation to him. The man just threw money at me and told me never to contact him again. Deeply insulted, I had no desire to find out via DNA if we were related– for fear we might be. I went to return the money, not wanting any part of the man. But something stopped me. I thought about my bullied mother and all she endured growing up without her father. It was the least she deserved. I decided to stay in the U.S. It is, after all, the land of opportunity, and I needed a career. The bribe money along with grants earmarked for Eurasians left behind from the war were sufficient to help me earn a nursing degree at a local college. I like caring for others. Helping them heal helped heal the broken things inside of me."

Faith felt foolish for acting like she was the only person who knew pain. Hers had been so all-consuming that it had blocked her skills of observation and caused her to focus everything inward instead of seeing what was right in front of

50

her. Looking outside herself might be a distraction and help to lessen, not intensify, the agony. "I'm sorry for assuming you could not understand."

"Please don't apologize, I share only to give perspective. I have not experienced as much physical pain as you have, but I know loss and rejection which is pain of another kind. Life experiences have taught me what I know and made me who I am. I wouldn't trade any of them. Well, most of them anyway. I wish I'd been able to save my mother. This life is but a journey to gather vast treasures of knowledge along the way. *To one who has faith, no explanation is necessary. To one without faith, no explanation is possible."*

Of course, he ended with a quote on faith. Faith almost laughed in spite of the pain. "I'm truly sorry, Tergar. I had no idea. I guess I need to come up with some Tergar quotes for you too."

"Good luck with that, and again no need to be sorry. I probably shouldn't have shared all I did, but I hope my story might help you believe you can also survive even the most tragic things."

Did it? Did she believe she would survive this awful experience? She may not have died, but could she actually live a normal life again one day? Tergar certainly seemed to have found the secret.

Chapter 8

Over the next several days Faith felt her anger slowly
start to slip away and take part of the pain with it. Her grief
was like an ocean, coming in waves that ebbed and flowed.
Sometimes the water was calm and sometimes overwhelming
enough to drown a person. She was trying to learn to swim in
this new ocean. Her doctors had ordered counselor visits to
help her discuss and process the stages of grief. Faith decided
it was time to let her guard down and let the therapist in if she
was ever going to get on with this thing called life and really
begin to heal.

A woman around her mother's age with soft, honey-
brown eyes and the same color of curls around her plain face
began daily thirty-minute sessions with Faith. Together they
determined Faith had already passed through the *denial and
isolation* phases of grief where it was natural to reject the idea
that all that had happened could be true. Faith had much to
absorb. Dr. Bodewell explained how we isolate ourselves to

avoid reminders of the truth. Others who try to comfort us may only make us hurt more while we are still coming to terms with the loss. Perhaps that was why she had been so harsh with those trying to help her.

Faith had just exited the *anger* stage. Once it was no longer possible to live in denial, she became frustrated and angry, feeling like something extremely unfair had happened to her, and she wondered what she had done to deserve it. The counselor gently assured Faith that life isn't fair; however, no one deserves to be badly burned in a house fire that kills one's parents. It felt good to leave the anger temporarily behind, but apparently, she still had more stages to look forward to. Dr. Bodewell felt if Faith was prepared, they may not be as difficult to traverse.

Bargaining was generally next where she would seek to change the circumstances of the situation causing her grief. It was an attempt to regain a sense of control as a defense mechanism against feeling helpless. A grieving person might seek to negotiate with themselves, the people around them, fate, the universe, or a higher power to change their circumstances. Bargaining might also look like ruminating about the details of the loss, seeking to understand or make sense of it, and wishing to go back and change the past in hopes of preventing the loss. Faith thought she had already attempted some bargaining and had dipped into the waters of *depression*, stage four, as well. The full weight of sadness and loss had washed over her on several occasions. Deep sorrow, anguish, and mental pain came and went in waves. The counselor helped her understand that feeling extremely down in the wake of a loss was normal; however, it was important to be aware that clinical depression is different from grief, and she needed to watch for it.

Eventually, Faith would or should come to terms with her loss when she arrived at *acceptance.* Accepting a loss did not mean she would no longer grieve. In fact, many grief experts say grief can continue for a lifetime after a major loss, but coping with the loss does become easier over time. Waves of grief might be triggered by reminders long after it happened and long after the person has 'accepted' it. These waves may also trigger a crossover into any of the other four stages of grief. Healing emotionally would be an ongoing process just like her physical one.

Faith was trying to take in and absorb everything Dr. Bodewell shared, but her mind often wandered around in tangents. She returned to this session in time to hear about one final and new stage of grieving.

"Some grief specialists have added a sixth stage of grief healing that I want you to be aware of, Faith. In 2019,

Kübler-Ross's co-author David Kessler published the book *Finding Meaning: The Sixth Stage of Grief.* In his book, Kessler chronicles his personal experience with grief after the death of his son and describes how moving beyond the acceptance of the loss often helps to find *meaning,* which in turn can bring hope and healing to the bereaved."

"At this point, I think acceptance is as good as I can hope for," Faith admitted. "I am not sure how anyone finds meaning in losing so many loved ones in an event that leaves that person alive yet quite disfigured."

"You are young and strong and bright; you might surprise yourself one day. You are still mourning. Mourning is sometimes thought to be interchangeable with grief, but it is different. Mourning is the outward expression of our grief. In other words, it is our shared social response to loss. In simpler terms, mourning is grief gone public. It is through authentic mourning that our grief begins to soften. After the loss of a loved one in our lives, we can feel torn to pieces or feel an enormous hole within us. You have a lot of holes to fill and are doing surprisingly well at this point in your recovery."

Dr. Bodewell patted Faith's uninjured hand before leaving the room. The woman did not appear to have any holes to fill. If so, they had been expertly plastered or grafted over. It didn't seem as if her counselor ever had a rough day in her life, but then neither had Tergar until Faith heard his story. Most people are probably dealing with something painful and challenging. Faith's visible burns just made some of her issues more obvious, but they were not the worst part of her pain or the biggest grief holes she needed to fill.

Looking around, Faith noticed several messages dotting her room which she'd previously ignored or was too oblivious to acknowledge. A warmth for the nurse who would not give up on her filled her heart.

"He who has faith has an inward reservoir of courage, hope, confidence, calmness, and assuring trust that all will come out well - even though to the world it may appear to come out most badly."

"Seeds of faith are always within us; sometimes it takes a crisis to nourish and encourage their growth."

"Faith is not simply a patience that passively suffers until the storm is past. Rather, it is a spirit that bears things - with resignations, yes, but above all, with blazing, serene hope."

"Faith in oneself is the best and safest course."

"For we walk by faith, not by sight."

Tergar was pretty amazing. Faith hadn't appreciated his efforts nearly enough. Housekeeping entered her room to empty the trash.

"Hey, do you happen to have a cell phone on you?" The hospital employee looked startled and a bit concerned. It was the first time Faith had acknowledged any of their presence in all the time she had been here.

"No worries, I'm not going to try to take it from you or make an unsanctioned call. Would you just Google something for me, please?"

The thin girl pulled a phone out of her pocket.

"Type in 'T-e-r-g-a-r quotes,' please." Faith had seen the spelling on his name tag.

"I don't see any quotes come up, but there is a Tergar Mediation App."

"Of course, there is. Does it say anything else?"

"It states their theme: *We treat everyone and everything as the embodiment of awakening.*"

"That sounds about right, thanks, that's all I needed." The housekeeper left the room looking confused, but the motto of Tergar Meditation made total sense. Tergar was awakening her, Faith, and her faith.

Chapter 9

Days turned into weeks; pages of the calendar flipped past a few months. Faith still felt like a freak, but she had to admit she could see improvement in her appearance, and she still had a few surgeries yet to go. Dr. Cope starting to talk about discharge was even more terrifying. She had missed the rest of the semester at college and could not see herself going back to the sorority. Superficiality largely based on popularity among the sisterhood of Greek symbols no longer appealed to Faith. A face scarred by burns would never fit in. Where would she go? What would she do? The thought was as frightening as her face.

Tergar showed up hiding an object behind his back. "I have a reward for you." He always seemed to know when she needed cheering up.

"Is that even allowed? Whether it is or not, I'm the one who should be giving you gifts." Tergar was constantly giving

Faith his time, his skills, his patience–and now he held an actual present.

"You gave me your first real smile this week, along with weeks of untiring efforts to get well. I would say you've given me plenty of the things that matter most."

"You are too good to be true, Tergar." Faith said the words in a casual almost flirty manner, but she knew they were honest and from her heart. The holiday season was nearing, but Faith didn't have an opportunity to shop or reciprocate in actual gift-giving. Once again, she would be the receiver. "Okay, let me see what you have there, Nurse T."

"I hope it is something you will love or at least like. I think it might be." Tergar pulled from behind his back a musical instrument that looked like a baby guitar.

"A ukulele! How fun. Now that my hand is almost healed, I can learn to play again, at least for myself. Not sure I'll ever play for others."

"About that. I have an idea."

"I could use an idea. Lots of ideas in fact. The doctor said I am going to be discharged before long and I have no idea what that will look like. I cannot see my life beyond the doors of this hospital."

"Okay, we can brainstorm. What are some of your possibilities?"

"That's just it. My future looks like a barren desert. I cannot see myself going back to college, and I'm not sure I still want to be a math major."

"What do you like? You seem to enjoy music. Have you ever considered that field of study?"

"I do love music and thought about studying it after high school, but decided it was not really practical as a career, even less so now. Can you see me performing on stage? No, thank you."

"What about music therapy? I could tell that you loved to listen to the volunteers who came and played to distract you from your pain. They weren't on stage; you couldn't even see them through your door."

Faith strummed her fingers across the taunt strings of the ukulele. A disharmonious chord erupted. This uke badly needed to be tuned. "I must get serious, Tergar. I'm sure my parents left me something, but it won't be much. I need to find a way to provide for myself."

"Music therapy is an actual career, Faith, with a degree and everything. I checked into it. The University of Kansas right near here in Kansas City has the longest-running music therapy program in the country. You may never get rich, but it could be super fulfilling. The flyer from the music department says a career in music therapy offers challenges, opportunities, and distinctive rewards to those interested in working with people of all ages with various disabilities. Music therapists are employed in many different settings including general and psychiatric hospitals, community mental health agencies, rehabilitation centers, daycare facilities, nursing homes, schools, private practice, and, as you know, burn centers. They can provide services for adults and children with psychiatric disorders, cognitive and developmental disabilities, speech and hearing impairments, physical disabilities, and neurological impairments. See, the opportunities are endless."

"You have my future all mapped out for me it sounds like."

"No, sorry. I just thought it might be something you would like and be good at. Being in a hospital yourself for so long gives you extra insights. You would know how to give comfort during a patient's worst moments. And maybe you could even work here. We could work together."

It wasn't a totally terrible idea. "Maybe. I will think about it. Thank you."

"You can choose for yourself, Faith. *Every tomorrow has two handles. We can take hold of it with the handle of anxiety or the handle of faith.*"

"Or hold onto the neck of a stringed instrument and make semi-melodic music. Now, do you have any sheet music for this little guy or should I keep randomly strumming chords."

"Chords are fine for now. I didn't think ahead. I'll find some music online and print off a few songs for you to practice."

"Thank you, I'd appreciate that. Can I ask you a serious question?" Faith continued to tune the instrument before she strained the air with any other harsh notes. "Why all the quotes on faith, besides my name obviously? What is it about faith?"

"Have you been absorbing any of the messages at all? Faith is what keeps us alive and helps us survive through all we cannot understand or make sense of in the world."

"What exactly is faith?"

"It is not a tangible thing. To have faith is to have confidence in something or someone. Faith is a principle of action or power and often grows from a tiny seed. Your mother gave you a great gift in your name which she told you is believing in something that you cannot see but which is real or true. You could be the literal embodiment of faith until you found your own."

"But faith in what?"

"That is a very good question for each person to decide for themselves. Some people place their faith in things that do not bring joy or are not deserving of their allegiance or faith. A person can have faith in pretty much anything. A lack of faith can lead to despair. True faith must be based upon correct knowledge, or it cannot produce the desired results. One's faith is a precious gift to give. The faith I speak of is in a higher power, one greater than ourselves who can see the future even when we cannot and knows what our lives can be. We hold onto their faith in us until we have our own in them."

"Are you speaking of Buddha? I investigated Tergar Meditation so know a little about what you believe."

"Buddha, Muhammad, Yahweh, Christ, the Supreme Being, the Almighty, our Creator, King-of-Kings, Lord-of-Lords, Alpha-and-Omega, God, our Father in Heaven are all good sources in which to place one's faith."

"Do you have faith?"

"I do, but I could always use a little more."

Tergar sharing his unfailing faith might be a more meaningful gift than the ukulele he'd just given her. The tuning completed, melodious music finally rose from the instrument's strings. Both gifts and the giver of them lifted her spirits and sang to her soul.

Chapter 10

Discharge day came far before Faith was ready. Tergar requested to be the one to wheel Faith to a waiting car upon her release. Her legs had always been fine, but it was hospital policy. She had intended to take an Uber to wherever she would be going, but an aunt, her mother's younger sister who lived only half a state away, had stepped up. Faith would stay with her Aunt Isabel, resettle into real life for a few months, and then start back to school at the University of Kansas in their music therapy program. Isabel and her mother had not been close, so her aunt hadn't been notified after the fire. It had taken Isabel time to discover that her sister had passed away, leaving behind a niece who needed her. Serendipitously, she found Faith in time to provide a home when Faith had none to go to. Tending to Faith seemed a way to make up for the time she had missed with her sister if that was ever possible.

Plans for college had fallen together quite swiftly after Faith–with Tergar's coaching–decided that music therapy was what she really did want to do. She had been called to create music all along. Math had merely been her fallback. The ukulele Tergar had given to her lay across her lap, and a small bag of personal belongings hung from the handle of the wheelchair. The open passenger door of her aunt's car awaited its occupant, while a beautiful bundle of fur named Cicero excitedly pressed his nose against the rear window and awaited her in the back seat. Isabel had rescued her dog from foster care, an insightfully thoughtful and greatly appreciated act by her newfound family member. But Tergar did not appear ready to send Faith away. Silence stretched between the two who had become friends–more than friends–over the past few months. Neither had a name for the relationship they had forged. Finally, after it really was time to let her go, Tergar bent over and gave Faith a gentle kiss on her healing lips, its sweetness enhanced by all they had experienced together.

"I have been wanting to do that for weeks."

Faith had never been kissed on her injured lips. The sensation was different, but the endearment meant even more. Faith had wondered if anyone would ever see her kiss-worthy again. The soft brush of Tergar's lips against hers brought tears to her eyes–and not from any pain. "Then why didn't you?"

Tergar grinned. "For two very good reasons. First, I wanted to keep my job, and kissing a patient is definitely grounds for dismissal. Then secondly, I knew I would be in for a slap across the face, if not worse, from my feistiest patient.

Faith smiled in acknowledgment. "You are probably right about that, and besides you had other things to work on before getting to my lips. I may still have scars that others can see, but you have massaged out and healed the most painful ones that circumvented my heart."

"*Your faith has made thee whole,* my dear friend. You know this is not a goodbye kiss don't you, well maybe a goodbye to patient Faith, but a hello to our future. It is the beginning of something more and different between us, if that is okay."

"I'd like that." Faith was too caught off guard to come up with more, so Tergar continued.

"*Faith is taking the first step even when you don't see the whole staircase,*" he whispered softly in Faith's left ear.

"Or" Faith added, "*When you come to the end of all the light you know, and it's time to step into the darkness of the unknown, faith is knowing that one of two things shall*

67

happen: Either you will be given something solid to stand on or you will be taught to fly. I think faith has become more than my name."

Tergar beamed down at his favorite patient. "I see that the pupil has become the teacher."

QUOTES on FAITH

We are twice armed if we fight with faith. Plato

*Faith is the bird that feels the light when the dawn is still
dark.* Rabindranath Tagore

*Be faithful in small things because it is in them that your
strength lies.* Mother Teresa

*To have faith is to trust yourself to the water. When you swim
you don't grab hold of the water, because if you do you will
sink and drown. Instead, you relax, and float.* Alan Watts

Faithless is he that says farewell when the road darkens.
J. R. R. Tolkien

*Faith is an oasis in the heart which will never be reached by
the caravan of thinking.* Khalil Gibran

*To one who has faith, no explanation is necessary. To one
without faith, no explanation is possible.* Thomas Aquinas

*He who has faith has an inward reservoir of courage, hope,
confidence, calmness, and assuring trust that all will come out
well - even though to the world it may appear to come out most
badly. B. C. Forbes*

*Seeds of faith are always within us; sometimes it takes a crisis
to nourish and encourage their growth.* Susan L. Taylor

Faith is not simply a patience that passively suffers until the storm is past. Rather, it is a spirit that bears things - with resignations, yes, but above all, with blazing, serene hope. Corazon Aquino

Faith in oneself is the best and safest course. Michelangelo

"For we walk by faith, not by sight." 2 Corinthians 5:7

"Thy faith has made thee whole." Mark 5:34

Every tomorrow has two handles. We can take hold of it with the handle of anxiety or the handle of faith. Henry Ward Beecher

Faith is taking the first step even when you don't see the whole staircase. Martin Luther King, Jr.

When you come to the end of all the light you know, and it's time to step into the darkness of the unknown, faith is knowing that one of two things shall happen: Either you will be given something solid to stand on or you will be taught to fly. Edward Teller

Burns

Burn wounds and injuries are often devastating. They can have severe long-term consequences for the victims, and they continue to be a major problem affecting communities worldwide. The treatment of these patients is often protracted, and large amounts of resources are needed to achieve the medical and psychological healing that needs to occur. Prevention is a vital factor that will have an impact on decreasing the morbidity and mortality associated with burns. Education and training are vital steps to empower communities to help them protect themselves. The most vulnerable of burn victims are children. Statistics from the WHO reveal there are over 300,000 deaths per year from fires alone, with many more from scalds, electrical burns, and other sources; however, there is still no accurate global data to confirm these numbers. Over 95% of fatal fire-related burns occur in low-and middle-income countries. Thousands of patients have survived their injuries but are often left disfigured and destitute. Children and the elderly remain the most vulnerable groups with the highest mortality. Intensive and specialized burn centers are in existence all over the world but are very often situated in high-income countries. These innovative and expensive treatment modalities play an important part, but the way in which a burn patient is initially managed carries an equally important role. Simple adherence to the basics including adequate resuscitation and meticulous wound care goes a long way to achieving favorable outcomes and even in influencing mortality rates.

RESPONDER SAFETY IS THE NUMBER ONE PRIORITY
1. Remove any source of heat including any clothing or jewelry in an area that may be burned, covered with chemicals, or are constricting.

2. If concerned about a hazmat situation, flush wounds with tepid water, avoiding hypothermia.

3. Cover the patient with a dry sheet or blanket to prevent hypothermia.

4. Assess airway/breathing. Carbon monoxide may present as restlessness, headache, nausea, poor coordination, memory impairment, disorientation, or coma. Administer 100% 02 as needed.

LEVEL of BURN SEVERITY ASSESSMENT:

• First Degree (Superficial Partial Thickness) •Red, dry, painful.

• Second Degree (Partial Thickness) •Red, blistered, weepy, swollen, painful

• Third Degree (Full Thickness) •Whitish, brown, charred, no pinprick sensation in the burned area.

BURN INJURIES THAT SHOULD BE REFERRED TO A BURN CENTER:

Partial thickness burns greater than 10% of total body surface area • Burns that involve the face, hands, feet, genitalia, perineum, or major joints • Third-degree burns in any age group • Electrical burns, including lightning injury • Chemical burns • Inhalation injury • Burn injury in a patient with preexisting medical disorders • Any patient with burns and concomitant trauma • Burned children in hospitals without qualified personnel or equipment for the care of children • Burn injury in patients who will require special social, emotional or rehabilitative interventions.

WORKS CITED

https://genius.com/John-hiatt-have-a-little-faith-in-me-lyrics

https://en.wikipedia.org/wiki/Tergar_Meditation_Communit
y

https://www.mayoclinic.org/diseasesconditions/burns/diagno
sis-treatment/

https://teachmesurgery.com/plastic-surgery/burns/skin-
grafts-and-flaps/

https://www.ncbi.nlm.nih.gov/pmc/articles/PMC3195355/

https://www.nowilaymedowntosleep.org/

https://grief.com/the-five-stages-of-grief/

https://www.musictherapy.org/careers/employment/

The Holy Bible, New Testament

About the Author

Teresa Meyerhoeffer Christensen has experienced all the elements of romance, drama, comedy, intrigue, tragedy, and adventure in over a half-century of earth living. She was born in Idaho to a basketball-playing, college president father, and cheerleader mother, who taught her to love to learn. She married her high school sweetheart, graduated as an RN, survived cancer, raised six amazingly unique children, taught religion classes for many years, was elected to the Bend-Lapine School Board while living in Oregon, and has served on various other boards in many volunteer positions. She now lives at over five thousand feet in Mountain Green where the air, as well as the veil between heaven and earth, are both much thinner and the inspiration plentiful. Teresa finally has the time to put down on pages all the stories that have been roaming around in her head for years. *Faith Didn't Die* is Teresa's thirteenth book. Jane Austen, T.S. Eliot, Henry David Thoreau, and Agatha Christie are all distant cousins. William Shakespeare was her twelfth great-uncle.

Website: www.TeresaMeyerhoefferChristensen.com